KT-555-658

Whistling Jack

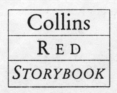

Other Collins Red Storybooks to enjoy

Harry, the Poisonous Centipede   *Lynne Reid Banks*
Max, the Boy Who Made a Million   *Gyles Brandreth*
Happy Birthday, Spider McDrew   *Alan Durant*
The Dancing Bear   *Michael Morpurgo*

Whistling Jack

LINDA NEWBERY

Illustrated by
ANTHONY LEWIS

CollinsChildren's Books
An imprint of HarperCollinsPublishers

First published in Great Britain by Collins in 1997
Collins is an imprint of HarperCollins*Publishers* Ltd,
77-85 Fulham Palace Road, Hammersmith,
London W6 8JB

The HarperCollins website address is
www.**fire**and**water**.com

7 9 11 13 15 14 12 10 8

Text copyright © Linda Newbery 1997
Illustrations copyright © Anthony Lewis 1997

The author and illustrator assert their moral rights to be
identified as the author and illustrator of the work.

ISBN 0 00 675295-0

Printed and bound in Great Britain by
Caledonian International Book Manufacturing Ltd,
Glasgow G64

Conditions of Sale
This book is sold subject to the condition
that it shall not, by way of trade or otherwise,
be lent, re-sold, hired out or otherwise circulated
without the publisher's prior written consent in
any form of binding or cover other than that
in which it is published and without a similar
condition including this condition being
imposed on the subsequent purchaser.

*For Alan and Arran,
in memory of a very hot day
at Stoke Bruerne*

CHAPTER ONE

Roger was a narrowboat dog. That doesn't mean that Roger was particularly narrow – in fact he was a little on the plump side. But *Whistling Jack,* the boat he lived on, *was* narrow. *Whistling Jack* was a long, low boat, thin enough to fit through the tightest lock gates and the narrowest stretches of canal.

Whistling Jack was rather an odd name, and Jack, the owner, often had to explain it to people. Whistling Jack was the name of a rare wild flower. Jack's wife, Annie, first saw Whistling Jacks on an island holiday – tall stems with pinky-mauve flowers. She liked the name so much that she used it as a nickname for Jack himself, because he often whistled a tune to himself, and whistled to Roger out on walks.

When they bought the narrowboat they had always wanted, *Whistling Jack* was the ideal name. Most narrowboats have paintings on their front and back doors, often of roses or castles. *Whistling Jack* had these, but it had Whistling Jacks too, painted by Annie, although not many people knew what they were.

When Annie was alive they had all lived in a tiny house in a big city, with the canal running past the end of the row of houses. *Whistling Jack* had been moored there, at the end of the garden. Every summer they used to set off in the boat for a few weeks: the three of them, Annie, Jack and Roger. But then Annie died. Jack missed her so much that he couldn't bear to live in the house any more. For a long time he didn't whistle at all, not even out on walks with Roger. Roger missed Annie too, but he tried to be as lively and bouncy as he could, for Jack's sake.

Then, after several gloomy months, Jack sold the house with all its happy and sad memories and now *Whistling Jack* was home for himself and Roger.

It was a moving home. One week it might be in London on the Thames, chugging slowly past Big Ben; the next week it might be out in the country, moored to a quiet river bank with only ducks for company.

Although it would have been better still if Annie had lived with them too, Roger liked his new life on the canals and rivers. He could pretend he was a real ship's dog, standing at the bow of *Whistling Jack* and barking when he saw a set of lock gates coming into view.

To show that he was ship's dog, Roger

wore a collar with a disc engraved *Roger* on one side and *Whistling Jack* on the other, with a little picture of a narrowboat.

Inside *Whistling Jack*, Jack and Roger had everything they wanted. The boat was not quite two metres wide, so everything had to fit neatly into its place. There was a tiny kitchen (galley, it was properly called) with a cooker, a fridge

and cupboards. Behind that was a sitting room and a table. Next came a mini-bathroom with a toilet and shower, and finally the bedroom, which had two bunks: the lower one for Jack, the top one for Roger. Roger slept curled up on a blanket, and his bunk was at just the right height for him to look out of the porthole window and see what was happening outside.

Everything Jack owned had to fit into the cupboards or in the spaces underneath the bunk and sofa. He even had a garden – flower pots in painted canalware on the roof and decks, filled with geraniums and petunias and ivy. He would water them each morning, and each evening as well when the weather was really hot. Every few days Jack and Roger needed to stop for water or fuel, or to buy food at one of the canalside stores.

On warm evenings in summer, when Jack had moored up, they could sit out on the deck while Jack did his crossword and Roger looked at the other boats going by. On cold winter evenings Jack closed the doors snugly, drew the curtains and turned on the radio, and brewed cocoa on his little stove.

Roger liked summer best, when he could lie on the roof and daydream, and when people walked along the towpath and admired *Whistling Jack*'s bright paintwork and the decorated flower pots. Sometimes they exclaimed to each other: "*Whistling Jack*! That's a funny name!" or "Oh, look at the little dog on the roof!" Roger liked attention. He knew that people thought he was clever, especially when he raced from one lock gate to the other waiting for the water to rush through. "You'd think he understood how it works!" people said.

Huh! Of course Roger understood. He'd seen it happening enough times. He knew more about it than most people did. He still found it exciting, though, when Jack opened the sluices with his special handle, freeing a torrent of water. *Whistling Jack*, waiting in the space between the two gates, would be lifted up by the water if they were travelling upstream, or lowered gently to the next level if they were travelling down. Roger liked to leap ashore as they pulled in to the lock, and he always knew exactly when to jump on board again, when the water reached the right level and Jack was ready to open the gates at the other end.

Often, they met people in hired holiday boats who got into all sorts of trouble at the lock gates. They'd lose their handles, or forget to tie up their boat when they got off, or have all the sluices open at once and then wonder why the water level wasn't right.

Roger didn't know how people could get themselves into such a muddle. It was simple, really, when you'd seen it done as many times as Roger had.

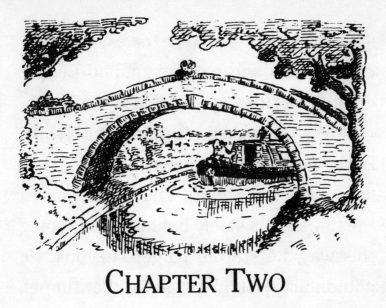

CHAPTER TWO

Hayford Lock was one of Jack's favourite places on the canal, because he liked going through the tunnel.

Jack and Roger were on their way from London to Yorkshire to visit Jack's brother. As Hayford Lock was a good place to stop for water and shopping, Roger wasn't surprised when Jack moored up there. It was a busy place, especially on a hot summer Saturday, like today. There were cafés and ice-cream stalls and a museum, and people could take rides up and down the canal.

Roger only liked stopping at Hayford Lock if they were travelling the other way, back to London. That would mean the tunnel was safely behind them. Going this way, he started to get nervous. He couldn't stop thinking about that tunnel, a short distance farther on. It was the longest, darkest tunnel Roger had seen, lasting for half a mile. In his imagination, it had no end at all. He thought of the entrance gaping like a huge mouth and throat, waiting to swallow him up.

Roger had been through the tunnel four times before, but he didn't think he'd ever stop being frightened, or understand why Jack liked it. Roger hated the dripping water and the echoey sound and the smoky smell – from the engines of all the boats that went through. So much water dripped from the roof that Jack had to put on his raincoat, even when it was perfectly dry outside. And it was so dark that Jack had to turn on *Whistling Jack*'s headlamp.

Even in summer, it was a cold, frightening place. Roger still trembled when he remembered the first time they'd gone through, even though it was more than two years ago. He had pressed himself against Jack's legs as the tunnel swallowed them up. Roger barked, and another dog seemed to bark back at him – a fierce, echoey dog, from somewhere in the blackness. Roger didn't dare bark again. He tried not to let the dark press against his ears too hard and he kept his gaze firmly fixed on the glimmer of light

at the far end, which slowly grew into a space big enough for the boat to slide through.

He was so terrified that he had nightmares about it for the next three nights.

After that, every time they went through tunnels, even short ones, Roger would slink down the steps, go to his bunk and curl up on his blanket, and wait for Jack to whistle to him when they were out in the open. Then he'd rush all the way from one end of *Whistling Jack* to the other, three times, and even (if it was a warm day) have a celebratory swim in the canal. Jack liked to see Roger swimming and would throw sticks for him to fetch, but he didn't like it so much when Roger showered him with cold water afterwards.

Today it was a *very* warm day. There were lots of people walking along the canalside, looking at the boats, taking photographs and waiting for rides. Roger tried to enjoy the holiday mood, and forget about the tunnel. Perhaps Jack would decide to moor up here overnight, and they wouldn't go through the tunnel until the next day. Or would that make it worse, Roger wondered – with more time to work himself up into a state of shivering panic?

Jack moored up, and he and Roger went into the canalside store for some shopping. Baked beans, a loaf of bread, a pint of milk, some chocolate and two tins of dog meat.

"Now for the tunnel," Jack said, knowing that Roger didn't like it. "We'll soon be on the other side."

Tail and ears low, Roger jumped aboard. Jack put the food away in the galley, then went to the rear of the boat to start the engine.

Waiting at the bow, ready to dart indoors as soon as the tunnel mouth loomed, Roger looked back wistfully at the crowded canalside, wishing they could stay a bit longer. Then he noticed that Jack had dropped something outside the shop door. The bar of chocolate! It would be a pity to leave it there, especially as Jack usually gave Roger a piece as a reward for going through the tunnel. Roger gave a quick *wuff* so that Jack would see what he was doing, then bounded ashore, ran over to the chocolate bar and picked it up in his mouth. The wrapper was shiny and slithery and he dropped it the first time.

He bent closer to get a better grip, picked it up, and turned to run back, expecting Jack to be waiting, pleased that he'd noticed.

Jack wasn't looking.

Jack hadn't heard Roger's *wuff* above the roar of the engine starting up. He had put on his raincoat, ready for the tunnel, and he was steering *Whistling Jack* out into the canal, away from the mooring. The gap was already too wide for Roger to jump.

He was left behind!

CHAPTER THREE

Roger dropped the chocolate bar and barked as loudly as he could. But Jack was steering away, waving to someone in a boat coming the other way and not looking back. He must have thought Roger was on his bunk, curled up on his blanket, ready for the tunnel.

Roger could easily run as fast as *Whistling Jack* could go – faster, when he was feeling really energetic. He left the chocolate bar where it was and started to run. But he'd hardly started when he collided with a fence of legs – a group of people walking towards him. One of them bent down and grabbed his collar.

"Wait a minute, dog! You've dropped your chocolate! You don't want to lose that."

Roger didn't care about the chocolate. The hand on his collar was kind but firm, leading him back the wrong way, back towards the shop. Roger picked up the chocolate bar and scampered off as fast as he could after *Whistling Jack*. But, as he rounded the bend, *Whistling Jack* was already being swallowed up into the circle of blackness. And there was no towpath through the tunnel.

Roger stood at the entrance and barked as loudly as he could. That other dog was in there, barking back. The dog with the fierce echoey voice was telling him to keep out.

"What's the problem, dog? Missed your boat?"

Roger turned round. Another narrowboat, *Tigerlily*, was coming slowly towards him, and a friendly-looking woman was standing on the foredeck, holding a mug of tea.

"Want a lift?" she called to him, and then she turned round and shouted to the man at the back who was steering. "Bill! Pull over a minute! There's a dog here that needs a ride through the tunnel!"

As the prow of the boat pulled over to the bank, Roger jumped aboard, dropping the chocolate bar at the woman's feet.

"Paying your fare, are you?" She laughed and bent to pick it up. "Thanks! OK, Bill, ready!"

Roger crouched on the floor. The front doors of *Tigerlily* were closed, so he couldn't dart in and find a comforting bed to hide on while they went through the tunnel. He would have to be brave. They would soon be through, and Jack would have realised what had happened and would have stopped. Even if he hadn't, they'd catch up at the next lock gate. They weren't far behind.

Tigerlily's headlamp cut through the darkness. Roger closed his eyes and thought about rabbits in sunny meadows. Cold water from the roof dripped on his back and ears and he tried not to think of that fierce angry dog who lived in the dark.

"Nearly there, dog." The *Tigerlily* woman didn't sound at all afraid – like Jack, she didn't understand what a dangerous place the tunnel was. Roger opened his eyes as the last bit of the tunnel slid over his head. The glare of the sun dazzled him. *Tigerlily* rounded a bend in the canal, and as his eyes cleared Roger saw, moored to the bank a little further on, *Whistling Jack.* It had never been a more welcome sight, with the paintwork gleaming and the sun picking out the Whistling Jacks along the stern.

Roger barked with joy, expecting Jack to be there, waving and delighted.

"That's your boat, is it? PULL OVER, BILL!" the woman shouted. "Off you go, then." She gave Roger a farewell pat on the head. "Don't get left behind again!"

As soon as *Tigerlily* drew near enough,

Roger jumped across to the foredeck of *Whistling Jack*. It was all quiet. The doors were closed and the padlock locked.

Jack was nowhere to be seen.

Roger's tail drooped with disappointment. Where could Jack have gone?

He jumped up and ran all the way along the roof, to check the rear deck. No sign of Jack. The doors at both ends were locked.

He ran back towards the tunnel, not knowing what to do next. Then he realised what must have happened. Where the black mouth of the tunnel opened, a gentle green hill rose above, with a footpath leading up to a level ridge. There was another way of getting from here to Hayford Lock – you could walk over the top. Jack must have realised Roger was missing and had walked back to find him.

On board *Tigerlily*, Roger had thought his problem was solved. But now he had a new one. He and Jack were at opposite ends of the tunnel!

CHAPTER FOUR

Jack had gone all the way through the tunnel and round another bend before he realised Roger was missing.

When *Whistling Jack*'s nose edged out into the sunshine, Jack whistled loudly and waited for Roger to appear from his bed in the cabin, bouncing with delight as he always did.

Nothing.

"Roger? Aren't you coming up?" he called.

Still nothing. Jack went down into the cabin and saw Roger's blanket, smooth and untouched since the morning. He searched the whole length of *Whistling Jack*. No Roger.

Jack tried not to panic. Roger would never run away, he knew that. Not even to avoid going through a tunnel. Jack tried to remember exactly the last time he'd seen him. They'd been together in the shop, he knew that, because someone had patted Roger and said, "What a lovely little dog! Such a clever face." And then they'd gone out, and he'd seen Roger jump aboard – he was sure of that. Almost.

Well, Roger certainly wasn't here now. There was only one thing for it. Jack would have to go back and find him.

It was difficult to turn such a long boat

as *Whistling Jack* in the narrow canal, so the easiest thing would be to moor up, lock the doors and walk back over the top.

Jack started off at a run, up the slope and along the top, above the tunnel. He wasn't awfully fit for running, and a painful stitch in his side soon made him slow to a jog-trot. Hayford Lock came into sight as he slithered down the steep bit at the other end. His eyes scanned the busy canalside. There were several narrowboats moored up, people wandering about, taking photographs and looking along the canal towards the tunnel, and several dogs sniffing around – but no Roger.

Where *was* he?

Almost in despair, Jack went from boat to boat, asking everyone if they'd seen a small brown and white dog.

"Yes – nice little dog with brown floppy ears? Saw him getting on another boat," said a helpful man who was filling up the water tank of a boat called *Marigold.* "About twenty minutes ago. Went on through the tunnel."

Jack felt weak. He couldn't bear the thought of losing Roger. Had Roger been kidnapped? Lots of people liked the look of him. Had someone thought he was lost, and taken him? But Roger had his name tag on – surely no one would try to keep him...

Jack tried to comfort himself. Roger was a clever dog – if he'd been kidnapped, he'd jump ashore as soon as he could. If Jack went back to *Whistling Jack,* he decided, Roger would probably be there waiting. He tried to cheer up.

"Want a lift?" the helpful *Marigold* man

said. "I'm about to set off, if you want to get aboard."

"Thanks," said Jack, and did.

CHAPTER FIVE

Roger decided that the best thing to do would be to wait. Jack would have to come back, sooner or later. He went as close as he could to the tunnel and waited in the shade of another boat that was moored there. He lay, nose on paws, looking towards the footpath. Jack would have to come back that way.

Up on the slope, a family had been having a picnic. While Roger waited they collected their plates and bottles and cartons and put them into a big basket, and walked down towards their boat.

"There's that dog again!" the boy said. "I saw him back at Hayford Lock."

"What's he doing by our boat?" said the girl.

The father walked up to Roger. "Good boy! Let's have a look at your collar." He looked at Roger's collar disc and read, "*Whistling Jack*. Oh, I remember. *Whistling Jack* was moored up back there by the shop. I noticed it when we came through. Thought what an odd name it was."

"We might as well take him back with us, if he's lost," said the mother.

No! Roger looked round and whimpered, trying to show them that *Whistling Jack* was just a little way round the next bend, not back at Hayford Lock

41

at all. But they didn't understand.

"Don't worry. We'll soon have you back on your own boat," said the boy. He lifted Roger in his arms and carried him aboard the boat, *Moorhen.*

"Put him down in the cabin, Kevin," shouted the father. "We don't want him getting away before we get there."

And Roger found himself shut in a room with bunks, like the one on *Whistling*

Jack but twice as long and with four bunks instead of two. The door was firmly closed.

He barked his protest, but the engine was already starting up. *Moorhen* had been turned round earlier and was pointing towards the tunnel and Hayford Lock. Roger jumped up to the porthole window to look out and saw only black slimy walls. He gave a mournful whine.

He hated being shut in. And, even worse, he was going through the tunnel again – without Jack, and his chocolate reward at the end.

At last the darkness outside changed to sunlight, and the door was flung open.

"Okay, dog. Here we are. Time for you to get out," said Kevin. He picked up Roger, who wriggled, wanting to get out by himself.

"That's odd," the father was saying. "Can't see that boat now. It must have moved on. Funny we didn't see it coming through the tunnel. I only saw that one other boat. Can't remember its name."

"I can. It was *Marigold*," said the mother.

"Now what?" asked Kevin. "What shall we do with him now?"

"Perhaps we'd better hand him in at the shop, and they can hang on to him till someone comes to collect him," said the mother.

No! Roger was going to find Jack by himself. He gave a furious wriggle, surprising Kevin, who dropped him. With one bound, Roger jumped from *Moorhen*'s deck to the shore, and rushed off along the towpath. He thought Kevin might run after him, but he looked back, saw the boy shrug, and knew he was safe. He'd escaped – now all he had to do was find Jack.

He expected Jack to be somewhere on the towpath, by the shop or the water-pump or the café. There were lots of people about and Roger ran from group to group, whuffling hopefully. But none of them was Jack.

"There's that dog again!" Someone was pointing. "That man was just asking

about his dog – isn't that the one?"

Roger ran past quickly, in case anyone made a grab for his collar. He told himself that there was no point in panicking. He knew what must have happened this time. Jack had come here, failed to find him, and walked back over the top. All Roger had to do was go back to *Whistling Jack*. He hid behind a café sign until *Moorhen* left its mooring and chugged off down the canal, and then he doubled back and ran up the steep slope over the hill.

He knew that Jack must be worrying about him! He panted, running as fast as he could, though he was beginning to feel tired with all this to-ing and fro-ing.

Only a few more minutes, and they'd be together again.

CHAPTER SIX

"There's my boat," Jack said to the *Marigold* man at the other end of the tunnel. "If you pull over I'll climb across. Thanks for the lift."

"No trouble," said the *Marigold* man. "Hope you find your dog."

Jack hoped so too! Carefully, he climbed over from deck to deck. He expected to see Roger waiting, paws propped up on *Whistling Jack*'s gunwale,

but there was no sign.

He whistled. He called. He searched.

No Roger.

Oh, no! *Now* what?

Marigold had pulled away, the friendly man waving, and the only person in sight was a fisherman sitting on the bank, between *Whistling Jack* and the tunnel.

"What's up, mate?" asked the fisherman, when Jack had walked past him five times.

"I've lost my dog," Jack explained. "Small brown and white dog, a bit plump, with floppy ears and a cheeky face."

"Oh, *that* dog," the fisherman said. "Gone back through the tunnel, on a boat called *Moorhen*. The family who found him thought he was lost."

"Thanks," said Jack, wondering what to do now.

Perhaps the easiest thing to do would be to take *Whistling Jack* back to Hayford Lock. If Roger was there, then they'd all three be together again: Jack, the boat, and Roger.

He got on board, unlocked the doors, started the engine and steered along the canal until he came to the winding hole. It was the only place wide enough to turn round.

Then he put on his waterproof coat and steered back through the tunnel. Drip, drip, drip, came the cold water from the roof. The boat felt very empty, because Jack knew that Roger wasn't there in his usual place on the bunk.

Whistling Jack wasn't the same without Roger on board. It was just a boat, not a home. Jack remembered what it had been like in the house, after Annie died – the rooms full of her remembered voice, the garden full of plants she had grown from seed. He *couldn't* lose Roger as well as Annie...

Jack could hardly stop himself from whistling when he reached the end of the tunnel, expecting Roger to come bounding up the steps.

Eagerly, he scanned the towpath at Hayford Lock. Surely he was going to find Roger this time!

CHAPTER SEVEN

Roger was hot and tired by the time he'd run all the way over the top of the hill. Panting, he padded down the last slope and scanned the canal bank eagerly. Then his heart sank. No *Whistling Jack*. There was only a mooring post where *Whistling Jack* had been.

Roger stared, blinked, and stared again. What had gone wrong this time?

He was so disappointed that he

flopped to the ground, nose resting miserably on his paws. *Now* what was he going to do? Had Jack got fed up with waiting and carried on?

No, of course not. Jack wouldn't do that.

There was only one person in sight – a fisherman, who stared at Roger with his mouth open.

"Well, blow me down! That dog again!"

He was sitting on a low stool with his lunch and his bait spread out beside him, but now he got up and came towards Roger. Roger watched him suspiciously. He'd already been caught twice today and he didn't want to be caught again.

"Come on! There's a good boy!" the fisherman coaxed, and held out a piece of stale bread.

Roger wasn't hungry and he didn't like

the way the fisherman was stalking towards him. He lay still, his eyes keen. Suddenly, the fisherman's hand darted out and grabbed at his collar. Roger bounded away, but the fisherman was more agile than he looked. Already tired, Roger didn't have much energy for a chase and the fisherman was close behind, a long arm reaching out. There was only one thing to do. Roger gave a yelp, launched himself into the air and plunged into the canal.

Wuuuuurghhhh!

The cold waters closed over his head and filled his mouth and eyes and nose.

Scrabbling, he rose to the surface, shook the water out of his ears and looked back towards the bank. The fisherman was there, waiting.

"Oi! Come back! I'm only trying to help!" he shouted.

Roger didn't dare to believe him. All he knew was that if he swam back to the bank, he'd be caught and taken somewhere he didn't want to go. He carried on swimming, doggy-paddle, looking back over one shoulder. And before he knew it he was swimming into the mouth of the tunnel.

He tried not to panic. At least the fisherman couldn't catch him in there. If he kept swimming he'd soon be back at Hayford Lock.

He didn't like it in the tunnel. He didn't like it even when he was safely on board *Whistling Jack*, and it was far worse now. The roof arched above him, dripping. The engine smoke that gathered in the tunnel filled his mouth and nose, choking him as he gasped for breath. The water around him was black and cold. And worst of all, there was that other dog in here, the one that barked and told him to keep out. He couldn't hear a barking dog at the moment – only the splashing water and his own panting. He was a good swimmer but he'd already been tired when he started, and now the tunnel seemed longer and darker than ever. As he doggy-paddled further in, the sunlight from the entrance faded, and he could barely see a semi-circle of light at the far end. He was swimming more and more slowly as he tired. Perhaps he'd never get there! He'd have to give up swimming and let himself sink, and then the fierce barking dog would be waiting for him under the water...

Fear made him swim faster, pressing his ears back so that water wouldn't splash in them. And then something

behind him filled the tunnel with golden light, so that he could see every seam in the brickwork and every watery weed that clung there. He looked over his shoulder. A boat was coming, its headlamp blinding him. A dark figure stood on the foredeck, pointing.

CHAPTER EIGHT

Jack?

No, the figure was too small and thin for Jack.

Roger swallowed a mouthful of water in his disappointment and kept swimming. The boat was gaining on him, and he heard a girl's voice call out, "Mum! Mum! It's a *dog!* A dog swimming!"

The engine slackened, and the dark figure was joined by another taller one.

"Fetch the boathook, Anna," a second voice said. "Quick!"

Roger didn't know whether he wanted to be rescued or not. While he was wondering, he felt the cold metal of a boathook slip underneath his collar, and the next moment he was pulled towards the boat and then lifted out of the water, dangling and dripping.

He could hardly breathe. He just had time to see the boat's name, *Anna Belinda,* and then he was plonked down on the deck. Water streamed from him, making a big puddle. He shook himself.

"Poor little thing!" said Anna, wiping herself down. "He must have swum in by mistake."

"He looks half-drowned," the mother said. "Take him below and wrap him up in a towel."

"He's wearing a name-disc, look!" said Anna. She lifted it and read, "Roger."

"Roger? I wonder if he belongs to that boat that's usually moored up by the third lock past the tunnel? You know the one – *Ringing Roger*," the mother said. "We'll stop as we go past, and ask."

No! No! Read the other side of the disc! Roger tried to signal with his eyebrows, but Anna only said, "Poor thing. He looks as if he's got a bad cold. I'll go and get him dry."

She took him down to the galley and wrapped him in a huge towel. Then she stood him on a bench seat and rubbed him energetically. Roger began to feel warmer and even a bit sleepy, but he knew he must *do* something – otherwise he'd be taken three locks down in the wrong direction and delivered to a boat

called *Ringing Roger.* Anna was kind, but he wished he could make her understand. She fetched him a bowl of bread and milk, but he took no notice, even though he was beginning to feel quite peckish. They were coming out of the end of the tunnel, into dazzling sunlight, and there, moored up by the canalside, was *Whistling Jack!*

Roger barked frantically and struggled to free himself. Jack was there, sitting on the foredeck with his head in his hands. He was just a few feet away!

Wriggling wildly, Roger tried to paw at the window to attract attention, but he was all tangled up in the towel. Before he could get himself free, *Anna Belinda* had slid past and Jack was out of sight. Roger gave a whimper of despair.

"Oh, you poor thing," Anna said. "You

really are hungry, aren't you?"

Roger stared at her and tried to shake his collar so that the disc would flip over and she could read the other side, but she only said, "What's the matter? Water in your ears? Never mind. We'll soon have you home and you can dry out properly in the sun."

"Anna! Come and help with the lock gates!" the mother shouted.

"Stay there. I'll see you in a minute," Anna told Roger, and went up the steps.

This was his chance! Roger knew about lock gates. Both Anna and her mother would be busy for a few minutes, and he could jump ashore. He scrambled free of the towel, jumped to the floor and ran up to the front deck.

The lock gates were ahead, and Anna was heaving the first one open. That meant that the water in the middle of the lock was already at the same level.

"The dog's got out," Anna's mum called from the back of the boat. "You'd better shut him up till we get through the locks."

"In a minute," Anna called back.

He'd have to be quick!

The lock gate was open, and *Anna Belinda* slid gently through into the space between the two gates. Now Anna

had to close the first gate and then wind the key to let water through the second, so that the water level would go down. Roger heard the gush of water as the sluices opened, and immediately *Anna Belinda* started to sink down as the water level lowered. The brick sides of the lock were just in reach, but if he waited any longer they'd be too high above him. He jumped up to the roof,

crouched, and sprang.

"The dog!" Anna's mum shouted. "Catch him!"

The brickwork was slippery. Roger scrabbled and slid back, hanging from his front paws. He mustn't let go! He kicked wildly with his back legs, heaved himself over the ledge and was up, panting.

"Here, dog! Don't run away!" Anna shouted. She ran towards him. Roger trotted over the closed lock gate and bounded off along the other side of the canal, as *Anna Belinda* sank out of sight.

CHAPTER NINE

Jack hadn't felt so miserable since Annie died. He sat on *Whistling Jack*'s foredeck, slumped and sad.

"I'll never find him now!" he thought. "He's been kidnapped, I'm sure of it!"

He had never felt so lonely. He didn't know what to do – he couldn't sit here for ever. But he couldn't face the thought of continuing without Roger.

Inside the shop, the shopkeeper had

been watching Jack for the last half-hour. Someone had told her he'd lost his little dog, and she felt sorry for him.

"Poor chap!" she thought. "He needs cheering up. I'll take him out a nice ice-cream cornet."

She went to the freezer, and made up an extra-large triple cornet of pistachio, walnut fudge and raspberry ripple ice cream. Then she stuck a chocolate flake in the top and went out to the towpath and *Whistling Jack.*

Roger, galloping back from the lock, had almost run out of energy, but the sight of *Whistling Jack* made him speed up. When he saw how mournful Jack looked, sitting there by himself, he managed one last burst, and launched himself on to the foredeck.

It was unfortunate that, just at that moment, the shopkeeper was leaning across the deck and holding out the extra-large triple ice-cream cornet.

Jack was saying politely, "Thank you very much, but I don't think I—"

Wham! Splat! Splurge!

Jack's mouth opened wide as a mixture of Roger, pistachio ice-cream, walnut fudge and raspberry ripple flew into his face. The chocolate flake flew into the air and landed on the towpath. Jack almost fell backwards into the canal, clutching Roger, who licked and wriggled in delight. He liked ice cream, especially raspberry ripple.

Twenty minutes later, when they were ready to set off through the tunnel, Roger noticed the chocolate flake melting on the towpath. He liked chocolate flake. It would be a pity to waste it.

No. Perhaps it had better stay there.

CHAPTER TEN

Soon after, still feeling rather dazed and amazed, Jack and Roger were ready to continue on their way.

"If only I could explain to him what happened!" Jack was thinking.

"If only I could explain to him what happened!" Roger was thinking.

Roger sat beside Jack on the aftdeck as *Whistling Jack* pulled away from the canalside. The woman from the shop waved, and Roger licked the last taste of raspberry ripple ice cream from his whiskers.

They would soon be at the tunnel, but Roger wasn't going down to his bed in the cabin. He wasn't going to leave Jack's side, not even for a minute.

Jack reached down from the tiller and patted Roger's coat. It was still damp.

"Well, I don't know what he's been up to, but he's certainly been in the canal," Jack thought, "and he's been through the tunnel at least twice. Even though he hates it. Perhaps he even *swam* through the tunnel? I wonder?"

He steered towards the tunnel entrance. Roger shivered a little, but stayed where he was, pressed against Jack's legs.

"I know what I'll do!" Jack thought.

"I know what I'll do!" he told Roger.

"Next time we get to a town, I'm going to find an engraver. And I'm going to get some extra letters engraved on your name tag. *Roger,* it'll say, *V.B.D.* That stands for Very Brave Dog."

Roger wagged his tail, so that it thumped on the deck. "It's almost as if he understands," he thought.

"It's almost as if he understands," Jack thought.

Not many dogs have letters after their name! Roger sat proudly, staring at the black mouth of the tunnel, waiting for *Whistling Jack* to slide in, out of the sunlight. He didn't think he'd ever actually *like* this tunnel. But he'd never be quite so scared of it again, not now he'd swum in it, and been through it in three strange boats.

After all, he was a Very Brave Dog now. And that's official.